For
Richard
Woods

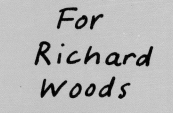

First U.S. edition 2001

Library of Congress Cataloging-in-Publication Data

Spanyol, Jessica.
Carlo likes reading / Jessica Spanyol.—1st U.S. ed.
p. cm.
Summary: Labeled scenes from a young giraffe's life—at home, at the market,
in the park, and at the library—offer opportunities to learn new words.
ISBN 0-7636-1550-1
[1. Giraffe—Fiction. 2. Books and reading—Fiction. 3. Vocabulary—Fiction] I. Title.

PZ7.S7368 Car 2001
[E]—dc21   2001025220

2 4 6 8 10 9 7 5 3 1

Printed in Italy

This book was typeset in Garamond BK Ed and Tekton Bold.
The illustrations were done in watercolor, acrylic, ink, and collage.

Candlewick Press
2067 Massachusetts Avenue
Cambridge, Massachusetts 02140

visit us at www.candlewick.com

CARLO LIKES READING

JESSICA SPANYOL

CANDLEWICK PRESS
CAMBRIDGE, MASSACHUSETTS

Carlo reads his bedroom.

Carlo reads his breakfast.

SHELL

SHOWER

Carlo reads
the bathroom.

BOAT

SPONGE

FROG

SPIDER

BUBBLE BATH

TOWEL

BATHMAT

FISH

LAMP

PICTURE

DADDY LONGLEGS

Carlo reads Dad.

FRUIT

RADIO

CATERPILLAR

PLANT

TABLE LEG

TAIL

CUSHION

WHISKERS

PAW

Carlo's mom reads to Carlo.

PUPPET

SPIDER

CARLO'S PAINTING

RABBIT

DOLLHOUSE

STRAW

STEGOSAURUS

CRACKERS

DRUM

CUPCAKE

HEN

ROBOT

PIG

Carlo reads to
Crackers the cat.

CLOUD

Carlo reads with his friend Nevil.

WALL

BUTTERFLY

PUDDLE

FLOWERPOT

WATERING CAN

LADYBUG

BACKHOE

PAIL

SNAIL

WORM

Carlo reads to a baby.

BABY'S MOM

BALLOON

OPEN

DOOR

BABY

BABY CARRIAGE

PACIFIER

WHEEL

Carlo reads to some ducks.

Carlo reads at the market.

RAINDROP

BEE

ROSE

SUNFLOWER

TULIP

DAISY

PETAL

PETE'S DOG

APPLES

CARLO'S BAG

Carlo likes reading very much.

And he loves galloping.

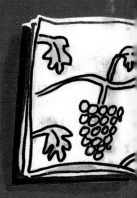